NO. IT'S PIGS

PIG the PUG ~~PUG~~ FIBBER

For my monkeys.

First published in Australia in 2015 by Scholastic Press,
an imprint of Scholastic Australia Pty Ltd.

ISBN 978-1-338-61219-6

12 11 10 9 8 7 6 5 4 3 2   22 23 24

Printed in the U.S.A.   76

This edition first printing, September 2019

The artwork in this book is acrylic (with pens and pencils) on watercolor paper.
The type was set in Adobe Caslon.

PIG the PUG FIBBER

Aaron Blabey

SCHOLASTIC INC.

Pig was a pug,
and I'm sorry to say,
he would often tell lies
just to get his own way.

And when he would fib,
he was awfully clever.
When Pig got in trouble . . .

he would always blame Trevor.

You see, he would mess up
the living room mat.

And then he'd just point and say,
"Trevor did that."

Or he'd shatter a beautiful
vase full of flowers . . .

And then he'd say,
"Trevor's been *crazy* for HOURS!"

He once even ripped up
a lovely old dress . . .

Your Special Day

Wedding D

Then he hid behind Trevor
and made him confess.

"Why do you do this?"
asked poor little Trevor.

"I thought we were friends."

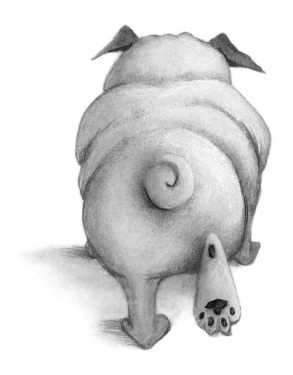

But Pig said, "Whatever."

Then came the day
of Pig's sneakiest plan.
He said, "I will steal
all the treats that I can!

They keep them up there,
in the closet up high.

But before I can get them,
I need a good LIE . . ."

And with that, he let rip.

It was stinky and grim.

Then he pointed at Trevor
and said, "IT WAS HIM!"

So Trevor was taken
outside for some air.

This was Pig's chance,
and he climbed on a chair.

"Those treats will be mine!
And *I'LL*
GOBBLE
THEM ALL!"

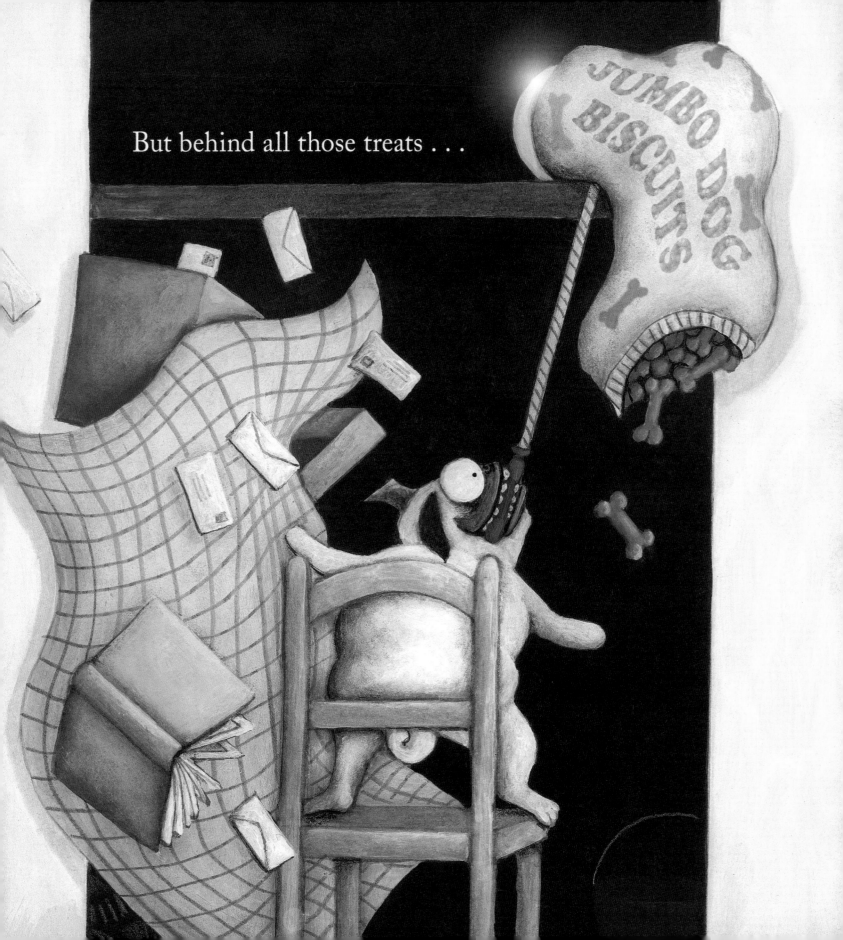

But behind all those treats . . .

. . . was an old bowling ball.

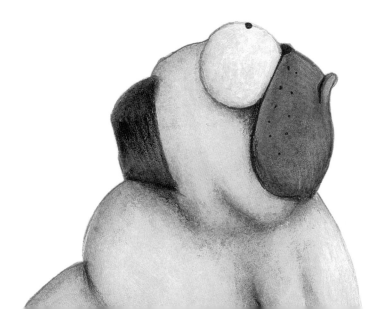

These days it's different,
I'm happy to say.
Pig has stopped lying!
Hip hip hooray!

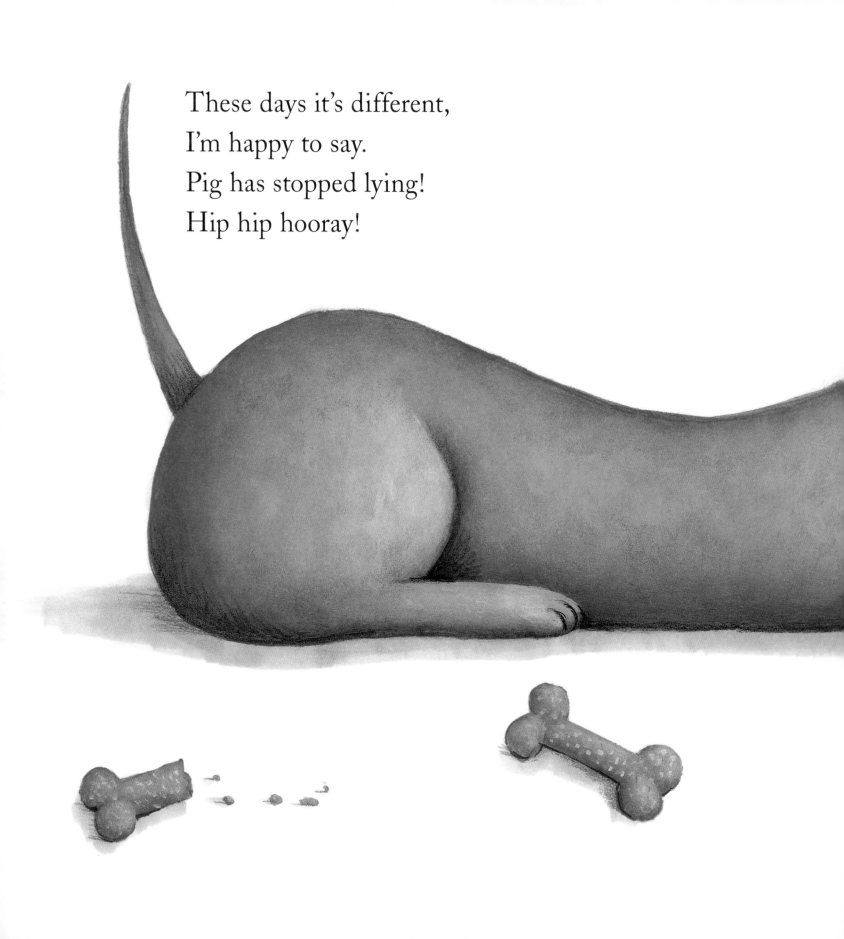

He may have some bruises.
And one less front tooth.
But he sure learned his lesson . . .

And that is the truth.